CONFIRMATIONS
—— OF THE ——
HEART

Library of Congress Control Number: 2015954700

ISBN: 978-1-63308-179-6 Paperback
          978-1-63308-180-2 Digital

Interior Design by R'tor John D. Maghuyop
Cover Illustration by Miša Jovanović

CHALFANT ECKERT
PUBLISHING

1028 S Bishop Avenue, Dept. 178
Rolla, MO 65401

Printed in United States of America

MYA EDWARDS

CONFIRMATIONS
—OF THE—
HEART

CHALFANT ECKERT
PUBLISHING

MADISON

M adison sat under the moonlight, penning the letters that she considered to be a lifeline to her soul; it was now a ritual for her. For years, her thoughts and emotions had been stifled but not anymore. The words came quickly and freely, as almost a divine release. And as the tears rolled down her face, her hand strong and steady, she breathed life into her words.

20 December 2010
Dear Babe,

Last night, I was screaming in my sleep. Schwabe was afraid to wake me because of fear it was a nightmare and I would punch her in the face...lol, I usually remember the important dreams the next day. Usually, there would be something in Earth's realm that would trigger my dream, but I never received any triggers.

But I did feel a shift in the spirit realm. The Lord usually wakes me up around 1 or 2 am; I shower and pray at that time (which are close to the times that the most spiritual warfare is being fought). I think the Lord always prepares me for war since I am a "spiritual warrior". I once asked GOD why must I fight for every freaking thing...and he said, "Because I have made you a warrior in my kingdom and that is your purpose. But don't dismay, you can never lose; you will always win because I will fight with and for you."

I asked GOD to tell me what I am preparing for and he said, "Don't worry, you are ready. I promised to never leave you and this is the reason why you were born. Although, I have impregnated you with many purposes, they have to be born in the right season.

The right season? Madison had wondered when the season would be right for her to receive all that God had promised. She had rightfully expected to be blessed one hundred fold and yet even as the letter slipped from her hand, the wheels were in motion. Destiny would follow, no matter what.

Then on the next day the letter came as easily as the first.

21 December 2010
Dear Babe,

I learned to be quiet today. I know you always tease me when you want to show off (who's in control) and say what does the Bible say about women? It bothered me how their lies about what I said (I know the reason). But I also know GOD fights my battles so I just love that fact that I am able to walk in truth. I admit occasionally I find myself wanting to lie, but for the most of it I really don't (John 16:13). I just keep reminding myself I am not fighting against the actual person, but the spirit (Ephesians 6:16).

Different people were arguing about the extra duty we have because of the squad leader leaving the hum v door open. But once again I did my best to keep my peace with everyone (Romans 12:18). Personally, I do find it easier to keep the peace because it seems the arguing and bickering will go on forever.

I've learned if you remain peaceful GOD will restore relationships. There were relationships in my life that were not peaceful, but the Lord changed all that (especially our relationship). I never dreamed that I would be here right now, at this very place, or moment with you. I remember how I used to feel: resentment, anger, disappointment, betrayal, hatred, etc. GOD has destroyed those feelings and filled my heart with a new love for you. I have complete peace.

So, I pray GOD gives you peace in all your relationships.

When she was done writing, she felt a kind of satisfaction, the same kind she always felt when she wrote her beloved, Terrence. Madison looked over the two letters she had written in the midnight hours, but she wasn't sure when she'd have a chance to give them to him. Instead, she stuffed them into her knapsack and pulled the flap over. The time for dreaming was over; it was time to work.

Today Madison fought with extra zeal, something she was sure she inherited from her own mother, who as it turned out, had been quite a trooper.

In fact, she'd always admired her mother's resilience, the way she worked hard and looked after the family, the way she never gave up even when the odds seemed insurmountable. As she thought about her mother, a tear came to her eye but she wiped it away quickly. Instead of crying, she would win and make her mother proud.

She scurried up the ropes, then over the large wooden wall, falling to the ground, with her heavy boots supporting her. She ran breathlessly towards some tires, being careful not to fall as she jumped in.

"Be careful," she heard someone shout.

She was blinded by sweat, but she still dropped hard onto her stomach, never minding that her bosom would be squished beneath her. It was a small price to pay. She crawled underneath the much too low fence, through the dirt and the mud then finally emerged, not so flawlessly as her shirt was hitched, ripping through her flesh and tearing.

"We made it," Madison said, trying desperately to catch her breath.

This was not exactly how she foresaw the end of the course, but training was always unpredictable, as was the battlefield, which she later found out. She knew she had to be battle ready. She stood up, placed her hands on her hips, and watched her team emerge. She studied their faces, one by one, and realized every soldier must be processed to be ready for war. In her mind here was no real alternative to training, and only the fit survived. Madison reminded herself what didn't kill her, would more than likely make her stronger.

Yet, even in her strength, she was human, but she also was a vulnerable woman.

Her memories reminded her of that daily. She was a woman stuck between two worlds—then and now, wishing she could go back and start over, wishing that her personal life was as orderly as her professional life.

TERRENCE

Terrence, on the other hand, was not so propelled by his emotions, but rather by his never dying need to persevere. It was the kind of stubborn tenacity only born leaders understood, something he had picked up from his father, his grandfather, and his grandfather's father before him. They were four generations of soldiers who never surrendered but fought to the finish. Terrence couldn't help it; it was in his blood. He would work day and night, remaining focused and stopping only to pray. As long as he kept going, moving towards the goal, he knew he would be okay.

Terrence also knew if he concentrated on his training and his works, which at this moment included finishing up the sixty pushups he was ordered to do, eventually he would not have to think about his feelings and emotions. Yet, sometimes even his discipline didn't really help him. Sometimes, in the quiet of the midnight hours, when all his fellow soldiers had gone and there was nothing left to do but think, he felt lost. Regrets plummeted him—things he had done that he regretted deeply and, for the life of him, he just could not figure out. And those things haunted him from the inside. Although no one could see these regrets, but those close to him noticed a hollowness in his eyes. He closed his eyes tightly, and he took a deep breath, trying unsuccessfully to forget her scent.

Terrence opened his eyes and whispered to himself, "A soldier must not feel. He must be null and void of all emotions, and he should be a good cadet."

It was a sacred mantra he believed in wholeheartedly. Yet, when he looked at her, love took over. He constantly fought to suppress his feelings, for love, life, and prosperity. That's just how it was, though, for a warrior. He looked around him at his fellow troops and felt a sense of comradery.

"Don't worry, men. We can do this," Terrence yelled at his troops, jumping to his feet with enthusiasm. He knew this was his purpose, and God had placed him on this earth to be a warrior. He would forever fight for life, love, and now land. Deep inside, he knew he must persevere, if he expected to be rewarded. He also understood it was the test that proved one's worthiness and produced the best there was.

"But our enemies look so fierce," one soldier said.

"The enemy is only as strong as we allow him to be," Terrence said.

Terrence was reminded of this in his own spiritual life. Every time he came up against giant situations, God had a consistent way of showing him, time and time again, that he could handle it, that he was really stronger than he realized. Now, Terrence knew he had the power to destroy his enemies, no matter what the circumstances looked like on the outside. He smiled to himself, knowing he had come a long way from being a fearful little boy to becoming a competent warrior, capable of building up or tearing down. God had put an awesome power into his hands and into the hands of the faithful, and Terrence certainly did not take it lightly. After all, with God on their side, what was there to fear?

Night had fallen around the now exhausted rookies, and they shoveled what was not much of a dinner into their mouths. Terrence noticed Madison had not come in yet; none of her squad members had returned. He shifted uncomfortably in his chair as he recalled his roommate telling him about his ear-splitting scream in his sleep last night.

"What was going on with you last night, man?" his roommate asked.

Terrence answered, "What do you mean?"

His roommate chuckled, "You don't realize that you were screaming so loud you almost woke up everyone in the barracks?"

"I kind of had the feeling that I was having a dream but," Terrence said before his roommate interrupted him.

"But you woke me up from a good night's sleep," his roommate continued, "and I don't get too many of those, given the circumstances."

Terrence wondered why he couldn't remember for certain he had been dreaming or what he dreamed about. What was it with him? Deep inside he felt like he had been dreaming, possibly something horrific but he could not recall, although he usually remembered the important dreams. This time there were no triggers in the earth realm to bring his nightmare back to the surface. He paced back and forth trying his best to recall but despite his dogged attempts, he couldn't. Not knowing what he dreamed bothered Terrence, probably more than it should have. He frantically searched his brain for answers.

Unfortunately, none came, and he was left with a desperate and incomplete feeling. He tried to shake it, but it wouldn't leave him.

However, Terrence remembered feeling a shift in the spiritual realm, and he awoke to pray around two a.m. that morning, which was almost routine. Every morning, about that time, he awoke with something heavy on his heart; it was always one thing or another. But, today, Terrence had a funny feeling something important was about to occur, so he drowsily prayed everything would be okay, even when he wasn't sure what he prayed about.

"Father, I bind all wicked spirits, powers and principalities, hindrances to your will of any kind, on earth as it is bound in heaven," Terrence had prayed, "And I loose peace, safety, the joy of the Lord, which is my strength, and all goodness that comes only from God on earth as it is loosed in heaven…"

MADISON

After the waiting and the worrying, Madison and her squad members finally arrived back to the camp, looking as though they had just been to war.

Terrence's squared jaw was rigid. "Where have you been?"

"What do you mean? You know where I've been," Madison snapped.

Madison refused to look in his direction and helped herself to some well-needed food, stuffing it into her mouth, as if she hadn't eaten in days. Indeed, she hadn't eaten well in days. Being in the camp had proved not to be the best environment for nutritious or pleasurable meals. Most of what she had eaten was hard and dry or tasteless. She could hardly wait to get back to home cooked meals.

When she was only six years only, her mother taught her how to cook. Madison was pretty good in the kitchen on most days. But once she put her mind to creating a culinary masterpiece, she was phenomenal. She remembered Terrence once teased her about becoming a chef, if she ever gave up her career as a soldier. He often told her he was amazed by her many talents.

It seemed like only yesterday the two spent the evening alone. Terrence sat at the dinner table waiting to be served, as Madison came out of the kitchen wearing an apron.

"Wow, look at you, all domesticated and everything," Terrence said, staring at her apron.

It wasn't a typical apron like her mother used to wear, but a contemporary version. Whether or not she wanted to admit it, the apron, a full one-piece red outfit trimmed with white lace and decorated with hearts, was sexy. Underneath the apron, she wore plain shorts and a T-shirt but from the frontal view, the shorts were barely noticeable. She remembered thinking the outfit would drive Terrence wild while she was cooking. *Lord, forgive me.*

Beaming with pride, Madison spun around, revealing the huge red and white lace bow tied in the back before asking him, "Do you like it?"

"I love it," Terrence replied.

He leaned back in his chair and gazed at Madison, looking her over again.

"I must admit that it's going to be difficult concentrating, though," Terrence said. His voice was husky, and Madison felt her cheeks blush unexpectedly. Terrence had a way of making her heart race with only a glance.

"I think you'll survive once you sink your teeth into my famous beef stew," Madison grinned.

Terrence shook his head, "And how do you expect me to keep my mind on food when you are so beautiful?"

"Hopefully, this meal will inspire you," she said, setting out a platter along with the other dishes and silverware.

Terrence pulled her close to him and sat her down on his lap.

He whispered into her ear, "You inspire me, not the food." Terrence kissed her gently and Madison found it challenging to pull away.

Finally, Madison managed to get control of herself and the situation. She hopped off of his lap and continued to serve the dinner, peering at him from her peripheral vision.

Terrence sighed, then said a prayer over the food.

"Thank you, sir, for the blessing," Madison said.

"No, thank you for such a wonderful evening," Terrence said before tasting his food and smiling. "This stew is the best I've ever had."

"It's my mother's recipe. She was always a great cook," Madison explained.

"I can believe that," Terrence said, stuffing another spoonful into his mouth.

"They say that the way to a man's heart is through his stomach," Madison teased. "Do you believe that's true?"

"I guess we'll just have to wait and see, won't we?" Terrence chuckled.

But as Madison's thoughts returned to the present, she wondered if her cooking or anything else had ever really gotten to his heart. And, if it had, how could he have so neglectfully toyed with and broken hers?

She slapped the dried mud off of her flushed cheeks as her squad members rambled around her, bickering about their extra duty and trying to exert their manly authority over her.

"All right, enough of that now," she said, quickly calling them back to order. She shifted past them silently and made her way to the table where she continued to eat peacefully. Finally, her nerves calmed and she was unflustered.

It had already been a long day; yet, she learned that humility and meekness were the best way. She decided she would not lie, but that she would, instead, be silent and let God take care of the rest.

TERRENCE

Terrence could hardly believe they were finally brought together again, sitting amongst each other, although not exactly together, sharing a common meal. After their last confrontation, there was a period of time he thought he might never see her again. Madison was so angry with him and unable to reach. After running into her by chance one day, he'd almost given up on her and counted it as one of his greatest losses. The memory still haunted him.

The supermarket was almost empty early the morning Terrence ran in to grab a gallon of milk for the cold cereal he forced down every morning for breakfast. Once he reached the dairy aisle, he heard a familiar voice to the right of him. Madison stood down the aisle. She asked the grocer a question about some of the fresh produce and moved about quickly.

Terrence fought the urge to approach her. As badly as he wanted to go talk to her, he was apprehensive. Carrying his milk like a lost puppy, he walked to a nearby row of shelves and pretended to make a decision between foot powder and jock itch cream. Finally, he collected his courage, and when she was finished choosing her fruit, he headed in her direction. With his heart racing and unsure what her response would be, he walked up behind her. Before he tapped her on the shoulder, he smelled the lavender in her hair. She felt his breath on her neck and seemed to know it was him before seeing his face, as she whirled around on her heels. Madison's mouth dropped open in shock at the sight of him.

"Hello, Madison," Terrence said, excited that her first reaction was not a punch in his face.

Considering what he'd done, he was ready for anything.

"Terrence," Madison said, acknowledging him. She looked him up and down.

"It's so good to see you," Terrence spoke slowly.

Madison glared at him, picked up her basket of fruit to walk away, and finally finished, "Is it?"

"You know it is," he responded. "Please, hear me out."

Terrence jumped out in front of her, careful not to touch her lest she screamed and made a scene.

Madison wasn't the dramatic type before, but he wasn't sure, if under the circumstances, seeing him so soon would've been too much for her.

"You'd better not block me. I don't have time for your foolishness, Terrence," Madison spat out.

Terrence looked down and sighed. "I completely understand…"

"Oh you understand, Terrence? What part do you understand? Is it the pain of betrayal you understand? Or is it the sheer embarrassment you understand? Perhaps it's the dishonesty you understand? Which is it, or is it all of these?" Madison finished and put one hand on her hip.

Terrence shook his head.

He said, "I'm sorry, Madison. I never meant…"

"No, don't tell me again what you never meant to do. Let's only talk about what you actually did. Let's talk about that, shall we?"

Madison circled him.

"Let's talk about how you slept with another woman or how you impregnated her, or maybe we should talk about the fact that you went as far as to propose to marry this woman. How many stab wounds should I be able to endure? Tell me, Terrence. Imagine my surprise when I found out you were engaged…" Madison finished.

"Madison, I…"

"Save it. Oh, and, I hear congratulations are in order, by the way," Madison said, as tears rolled down her face. "Have a spectacular life. I hope you're very happy together, the three of you."

The confrontation had been raw and bitter, and the tragic end of a beautiful relationship. And it was all his fault. Terrence knew he had been stupid and weak and now he lived with his punishment. There was nothing he could do to rectify it. Everything he'd believed in was lost—the love of his life and all of his hope for the future. He was caught between obligation and true love. Since the beginning, he wondered what was the right thing to do.

After much prayer and meditation, he had heard the word *marriage* in his spirit. His flesh hadn't agreed; he'd wanted Madison. *What was this sacrifice God was asking of him?*

He would have to give up sweet Madison completely, even his dreams of her. The only thing left would be semi-washed away memories of what was once one of his greatest joys. And in doing this, he would have to give up a part of himself to secure a part of himself, the part of him who was Jeremiah, his son.

Jeremiah deserved so much more than he had growing up. Terrence wanted to give him a stable home and an intact family, something he—a product of divorce—never had. He wanted Jeremiah to be showered not only with the love of his two parents, but also he wanted to raise him up and give him back to God. Much like Hannah gave her only son, Samuel, and like his heavenly father gave his son on the cross, Terrence wanted his life as a father to be a sacrifice. He wanted to be a good example, even if it meant denying his own needs, even if it meant holding his own heartache.

For more than a year, in secret, Terrence cried and endured the mockery of his family. But once he realized that fate had intervened and linked him and Madison to the same military operation, he was happily surprised. It was as if his heart opened up again—old wounds and all.

Terrence's heart flustered when finally she lifted her gaze from her dinner plate and looked at him. He expected a scowl or even a glare, but instead she smiled at him. Surprisingly, it was a genuine, peaceful smile. Was it possible Madison really forgave him?

Madison's face shined with a surprising peace, and he wondered if God had made her whole again, obliterating all the hurt and resentment toward him. He imagined that perhaps she was filled with a foreign kind of love for him. Terrence returned the coyest smile he could muster up. He was relieved to see her glow at him like she used to, but he was still anxious to see what was ahead. Terrence was uneasy and his heart was completely vulnerable. He sensed a change and, although God implored him to welcome it, he was afraid, afraid that even together they would not be able to handle it.

22 December 2010
Dear Almond Tree,

We have the confidence to ask GOD for anything and trust that he can do it (Matthew 7:7). We know keeping GOD first prioritizes getting things added to us (Matthew 6:3). But we don't want anything that is not His will. That's why we pray, "Let your will be done." Sometimes, I am anxious about my prayers being received and answered, but that is when patience comes in (Philippians 4:6).

I sometimes think we pray for things we can't handle, will make us struggle, or just not the right timing. So GOD steps in on our behalf and gives us what we can deal with.

So I pray that you go to the Lord and let your petitions be known to him in his will. GOD wants to bless you so he will make a way for you. Rely on his strength and continue to serve the Lord with all your heart. While you're living every day, wait expectantly for GOD to help you daily.

23 December 2010
Dear Babe,

Exactly three years ago today, I prophesized to you. God told you that your wife would prophesy to you, and he told me some things about you. We ended up talking on the phone over a day. Those years still feel like days gone by to me and not years. The enemy tried to bring up old negative feelings I had then, but I refused to let them surface. Those things in the past can't hold us back anymore, because GOD has declared "new things" in the Spirit. When GOD speaks he makes his purpose clear (Isaiah 48:2-4).

Perhaps, I look younger than my age, so I am able to relate to the youth. Maybe, I had to be older than you because there are things I had to teach you. GOD answered my prayers when I said I wanted to be established before getting married and having children. Now, you can go to school to get your degree, and I can help you. It is possible, since I am in the military, here with you now because I prayed for us to be unified. Since I am your spiritual wife, it is my job to be a helpmate in everything you need. But why did God allow you to marry her? If I am truly your wife, spiritually and on this earth…why did He allow this to happen? I always believed God's promises and still do.

When GOD spoke us into existence, our purpose was already fulfilled. We just need to walk out the process to get there. GOD's word doesn't return to him without accomplishing his purpose (Isaiah 55:10-11). He speaks it and it comes to pass because the word is made flesh (John 1:14).

So I pray right now in the name of Jesus that we leave our past behind, so we can look toward a new future together. Lord, continue to make "new things" in our lives where we can give you all the glory and remind us not to limit you in any way. I declare we continue to walk out our process to get to our purposes in Jesus' Name Amen.

MADISON

Madison stole glances at Terrence from afar, careful not to arouse any suspicion whatsoever, as to the nature of their relationship. And what was the nature of their relationship? Wasn't he now a married man, no longer belonging to her, no longer free in expressing his love for her? As she saw him coming, she looked away, not wanting to appear desperate. Her heart beat faster though, as he approached her and sat down.

"How are you?" he asked in his deep, sultry voice.

"I'm good," she said, trying to be calm but she was drawn to him. "But we must be careful. The danger is not over yet."

"God will be with us," he said, with his eyes fixed on her, making her feel uncomfortable. How could he bring up God at a time like this, when all that she could think of was

sinful? His smell was musky and masculine as always, and she missed the way it tantalized her nostrils. Terrence stood in front of her just close enough to be touched; yet, she didn't dare reach out to him. Yes, their relationship was a strange one, but, nonetheless, it was one that she wasn't willing to give up. *God, help me.*

TERRENCE

Terrance lingered over his vows as he took caution in making sure the next thing he asked God for would not be something he would later regret. He didn't want to have to toil through magnificently or be faced with a series of obstacles. So he decided to turn it all over to God. He prayed for Madison, as he always did. However, in the middle of his prayer, he paused to think about all of the distress he had caused her over the past few years. He also thought about how much she now struggled to find peace. He didn't know for sure, but he could see it in her eyes every time she looked at him.

Madison always had a way of getting to him. He sighed wearily, digging a tad too much into his bronze skin, which was blistered and red mostly from the effects of training and now his vigorous scrubbing. Tonight he knew he would immediately fall into an exhausted coma the moment he hit the mattress. He let his mind wonder for a moment, as the cascading crystals from the shower head exploded on his back and into his hair. He was anxious awaiting God's answer. A piece of him hoped God would answer his prayers and another piece knew he needed to be patient.

Constantly, Terrence rehearsed comforting scriptures, which turned out to be constant reminders. Was it wrong to tell God the way he felt, to pour out his heart and disappointments at the throne of the Almighty? Right or wrong, Terrence found himself on his knees.

"Lord, I know that I shouldn't, but I miss Madison so much. I still see her face in my dreams. I still hear her voice as I sleep. She's a part of my heart, and I can't cut her out, although I've tried. How do I remove myself from what I am feeling? My flesh tells me one thing, but my spirit tells me another.

But I know there is more at stake than Madison. There is my marriage to Monique, the future of my precious son, Jeremiah, and your will for my life. Ultimately, I want to be in good standing with you and have my name written in *The Lamb's Book of Life*. No matter what I go through, Lord, don't let me out of your hands; keep your hand on my life, and I will gladly obey. Give me your word, and I will rejoice in it.

But I can't go on this way. Please take away this longing I feel. Take away the taste and the touch and the smell of her that is implanted in my mind. Take away her words that have found a place on the inside of me. Take it all away, Lord, for your glory. I pray that I may find mercy and forgiveness at your throne of grace, Lord. Amen and Amen."

Terrance winced when he felt the sharp sting of a wet towel bite into the flesh of his naked white buttocks, waking him out of his trance. Laughter bounced off the walls of a six-foot-two-inches tall, handsome African American man who looked away innocently. It wasn't long until the men would be dispatched and all gimmicks would not involve towel slapping. This bothered Terrance, and, although he was annoyed by their taunting, he laughed to himself, savoring the precious moments he had left with his friends.

And so, the last few words Terrence uttered before draping the towel around his waist was that he would survive, not only for himself but for Jeremiah and Madison.

"If it is God's will, let it be done," he mumbled to himself.

He exited the showers and walked into the locker room, reassuring himself that God would protect, guide and nurture his soul mate. *Soulmate.* He rolled the words over in his mind and fretted about them. He wondered if he should he even feel this way about Madison, given his commitment to another.

His *soulmate*, he whispered to himself before falling asleep.

MADISON

Madison collapsed from exhaustion onto the floor, releasing a single breath of air as her now feeble and aching arms trembled underneath her. She completed one-hundred and fifty push-ups for not responding alertly enough when her sergeant addressed her. Her sergeant called her name thrice before she responded, and, although Terrence looked as if he felt sorry for her, there was nothing he could do to save her.

Madison looked straight at him as if she was looking right through him, beyond him. Her mind drifted off deep into thought, reminiscing, reflecting on the past they had together. She stood erect, arms behind her back, shoulders back, head straight, aligned, in sync with the rest of her teammates. Yet, she was not so in sync that she wasn't distracted by a saddening memory.

It was a memory of the man she loved wedding another woman. It was the most painful memory of her life. She scurried through her mind trying to see how best she could find the silver lining. Then just as she was about to be overwhelmed by grief, God slowly began to put the phrase "blessings in disguise" into perspective. Madison thought about how if it had not been for the past few occurrences, she and Terrence would not have been reunited there in the Army.

Madison would not have realized the beauty and the true worth of her age and wisdom. She also would not have been given the opportunity to impart all she had learned and experienced in grooming, guiding, and teaching the man she loved. She wiped away the tears that had found their way down her cheeks. She closed her eyes and took a deep breath, deciding to ignore the ugly stumbling blocks. In her heart, she chose to believe she truly belonged to Terrence, that they were destined to be, and that she would take care of him in every way she could.

"I refuse to let the past get in the way," she resolved and declared to herself, just as she finished all one-hundred-and-fifty pushups flawlessly.

Madison was determined that with God's help, she and Terrence would press on despite their tumultuous past.

24 December 2010
Dear Babe,

Merry Christmas, Can you imagine what the spiritual realm was like before Jesus was born. We know the preparation for his birth was saturated with holiness (Luke 1). GOD sent his holy angels to bring messages to prepare his people. Zacharias was visited by a holy angel and it declared even his son would be filled with the Holy Spirit in his wife's womb. So perhaps, Jeremiah is filled with the Holy Spirit too.

Gabriel visited the Virgin Mary telling her how she would conceive and bring forth Jesus Christ. Then Mary visits Elizabeth, who is already with child as well when Mary meets her, then her baby leaped in her womb. Next, Elizabeth was filled with the Holy Spirit.

Terrence, so when the Holy Spirit shows up everyone is overwhelmed by its power. It's because we have the Holy Spirit inside us, that we must connect so it can be complete or one. I think we underestimate how power the Holy Spirit is and how much power we have because it lives in us. I feel a crazy faith level about to take place and GOD has prepared me. Thank you, Lord, for making us prepared vessels.

I pray that the GOD of hope fills you with a new knowledge of what the Holy Spirit is and can do in your life. I ask the Lord to give you joy and peace in every situation. I pray that you trust in him at all times. Lord, I intercede for Terrance, that you give him an overflow of hope and power of the Holy Spirit (Romans 15:13). In Jesus' Name Amen

TERRENCE

Terrence remembered vividly the night his whole life fell apart. He had been at home visiting with his family and had stopped to collect the mail. He anxiously tore it open as he entered the kitchen, forgetting he was in the company of doubters. His family not only doubted his relationship with Madison, but they also doubted his ability to make mature and rational decisions. Perhaps, being the youngest of his siblings had brought him to that point.

"Another letter from Madison?" his mother asked and approached him with the most distasteful scowl.

"Yes," he responded, matter-of-factly.

Terrence didn't look up from the wrinkled diary leaf. He already knew the look of displeasure that was plastered across his disapproving mother's face. His mother stood with her arms folded across her chest and tapped her foot on the tiled floor. Terrence waited for her comment, but instead she left the room. He let go of the breath he was holding on to, whispering a silent prayer as he did.

He stood on the porch and inhaled deeply, suddenly being filled with a sense of satisfaction, a divine contentment he could not understand.

"She's too old for you," his youngest sister said.

"What does age have to do with anything when we are both consenting adults?" he said.

"Consenting? Consenting to do what?" his youngest sister mocked.

Terrence frowned. "The truth of the matter is that we're adults and that is none of your business…"

"That means they're doing something they shouldn't out of the will of God," his oldest sister said.

"Look, you don't know anything at all about the will of God. I would watch it if I were you," Terrence said, sternly.

The oldest sister chuckled. "Are you threatening me, baby brother?"

"I am merely stating the facts. You don't know anything about our relationship or our lives, much less the plans God has for us," Terrence continued.

"But what can you see in her?" the youngest spat out.

"She is beautiful, sensitive and intelligent. Terrence's eyes darted from sister to sister.

"And you couldn't find that in someone closer to your age?" the youngest sister continued.

"Nevermind about that, but she's rude," the oldest sister chimed in.

Terrence raised his eyebrows. "How is she rude?"

"She's very uppity, always strutting in and out of the church like she's too good for everybody else," the oldest one explained.

"That's not true. She just likes to keep to herself sometimes; that's all."

The oldest sister smirked. "Is that so? I see she had no problem attaching herself to you, though…"

"Oh, this is ridiculous. I don't have to defend Madison to you all." Terrence rolled his eyes.

His second oldest sister added, "What does she want from you anyway?"

"Maybe she wants his body," the oldest one said and burst into a fit of laughter.

The other two joined in until he couldn't take it anymore. He had to get out of there.

Given their inciteful comments, he was grateful his mother had already left the room. He had spent so much time listening to them hurl insults and give him lectures on the right way to have a relationship as if any of them had a clue. With no disrespect intended for his mother, but she had not been with his own father in many years and neither of his three sisters had husbands of their own. What could they tell him about love unless they'd experienced it for themselves? And as far as he could tell, love had been as far from their lives as the east is from the west. But he was not one to want to hurt their feelings so he held his tongue.

He pushed the front door open and scurried past his criticizing family, ignoring their comments about the strange love affair...

"She's nothing but a cougar," his older sister continued.

"I'd say a pedophile...," his mother scoffed as she reappeared on the scene. Never mind that he was twenty-five, old enough to date and love whomever he pleased; Terrence was livid.

'Damn,' he thought, and crumpled the letter between his fists and tried desperately to contain his rage. He buried the note in his pocket and stormed out of the house, out of the yard and into the street. No amount of Christmas carols could penetrate the hurt and the annoyance he felt. Yet, the stubborn carolers sang on, and the stubborn Christmas lights flickered, and the kids in the old man's yard still laughed and clobbered each other with snowballs.

'Damn,' he thought again, quickening his pace. He remembered his friends' distasteful reaction when he revealed to them that he loved Madison, and it enraged him. It seemed that no one understood him, and no one was willing to listen. Having nowhere to really turn, he ran. He ran from his family, from his emotions and from himself; but, of course, there was no escape.

Breathlessly, he stopped at the end of what must have been the sixth or seventh block. He coughed and heaved, with his eyes fixed on the pavement.

"Here, have something to drink," A small, all-too familiar voice offered. He looked up; it was his high school sweetheart, Monique. Instead of going to his own apartment, he realized he must have subconsciously ran all the way to her front yard.

She stood before him, looking as beautiful and as innocent as ever. For a moment, he struggled to remember why they broke up, but that had been so long ago it wasn't even important.

"Thank...you." He was reluctant but thirsty, so he took the drink and chugged down the yellow liquid.

"Wow, this is good," he commented as he struggled to find his breath.

"There's more where that came from," she said, pointing to the house. She touched his arm, compassionately; then she looked at his face and smiled, intently.

"You look like you need more."

A concerned scowl grew across her temple, then she dried his face with her sleeve.

Terrance was unaware he had been crying and the revelation frightened him. *What's happening to me?* When he looked up, he noticed that Monique was wearing a low-cut, fitted sweater and a thigh high skirt which exaggerated all of her curves. She leaned in close to him, and he could feel her breath on his neck. He backed up a little, but she kept coming closer.

"Come inside and we'll talk about it. No one should have to be this way during the Christmas holidays," she whispered in his ear, consoling him. "It's okay. I understand." Then she pressed her voluptuous body up against his and signaled him one last time.

He succumbed to her invitation, which facilitated the perfect vacuum to expel his conflicting emotions, his hurt, and his rage and with that, he betrayed the woman he claimed to love.

Terrence winced at the memory, and then put the final touches on the gift he was wrapping for Madison. He was afraid a little part of him regretted that his son, Jeremiah, was conceived, and that he detested what happened that Christmas Eve. Then he remembered Madison's letter about how Jeremiah may be filled with the Holy Spirit. This made him smile, and he hid the gift beneath his pillow.

"Yo Terr, the guys 'bout to put the finishing touches on the tree. Are you done with your decorations?" one of his squad members asked.

"Uh, yeah..." he grabbed both the decorations and the gifts and proceeded to the cafeteria, a now brightly decorated and well-illuminated place with a large tree standing in the midst. He sighed, put his gift beneath the tree, then hung his ornament, a large sea shell with the phrase "...So the Holy One to be born will be called the Son of God" carved into it.

He hated that the holidays could take his mind back to that awful night of passion, the night he had betrayed his one true love. *Lord, why have you allowed me to sin against you and against Madison?*

25 December 2010
Dear Babe,

I got a third gift today and included was everything I wanted. I especially loved the photo album of memories. I sometimes think we lose sight of the meaning and what is a "gift." GOD gave the greatest gift of all and yet we still don't understand the meaning of gifts (John 3:16). We don't understand who we are in Christ. But the Lord said he made us a little lower than angels and crowned us with glory and honor. How special is this privilege!

So, Lord, I praise you for this day, for giving us the true gift, for making us in your image and glory of you (I Cor 11:17). I pray that you make Terrence complete in you and head of all principality and power (Col 2:10). Give him peace, security, and acceptance by you. Free him from any imprisonment spirit that wants him to forget who he is in Christ and the gifts that are given to him, in Jesus' Name. Amen.

"Hey, Madison." The tall, dark, slender woman strolled towards her. She draped her bronze ponytail across her shoulder, immaculate and braided like it usually was.

"Yes ma'am!" she responded dryly.

"At ease soldier." She stifled a laugh.

"I just wanted to tell you…mhm…Merry Christmas, kid," she said, a half-gentle smile forming across her lips.

Madison smiled back at her. "Merry Christmas to you too."

With that, the woman handed her a parcel. "I believe this is yours."

"Oh no no…you didn't have to." Madison was reluctant to accept the gift.

"Well, I thought why not? It was the only thing beneath the tree and I figured you didn't know it was there."

"Oh... it's...not from you?" she inquired, then blushed at the misunderstanding.

The woman laughed and handed her the perfectly wrapped and colorful package. "Naw, I'm just the delivery person," she said, then turned to leave.

Madison turned the parcel in her hands before tearing the greeting card from it.

'FOR YOU.... LOVE'

Was that all it read? Madison swallowed hard, as all kinds of images popped into her mind.

The woman stopped at her doorway and faced her. "Hey...why don't you go home, Madison? You've got your leave; you deserve it...No one should have to spend Christmas in a training camp of any sort. Come on. I'm sure your family misses you."

"No! I'm sorry, ma'am...I just.... It's not necessary, but thank you. Enjoy your holiday Sergeant." And with that she mustered up the most genuine looking smile she could as she fought back the tears that threatened to burst from her eyes.

"I understand; thank you, soldier," she returned a warm smile and left.

Madison took a deep breath as she sat on the edge of her bed, softly. She stared down at the brightly colored gift in her hands, then looked over at the other two gifts she had received from friends that were sitting beside her. Why did he continue to have this effect on her?

She put Terrence's gift down and decided to open the other gifts first, saving his for last. She tore at the packages. She received a small angel carved out of a straight-grained, reddish-brown sweet wood. It resembled mahogany. However, she doubted that very much. Suddenly, the empty loneliness she felt inside earlier slowly melted away and she picked up her other gift; it was a black, knitted sweater. She smiled as she looked back to see if Terrence was anywhere near.

"Those are nice gifts," someone said.

"Yes, they are," Madison agreed, holding the sweater in front of her.

Then she noticed the words, 'Merry Christmas Soldier' embroidered on the back. Unable to contain herself, she burst out laughing. She pulled the sweater over her head to try it on and to model it for her teammates.

"Looking good, soldier," one woman said.

Finally, she picked up Terrence's gift and sighed. Feelings of love, guilt, and anguish all filled her at once. She braced herself for what she was about to see.

Terrance had gone home to his family, his wife, and child and she was left to deal with that. . She recited a prayer in her head for him while she slowly ripped at the paper that wrapped the gift. Then she began to smile from ear to ear as she realized he still cared.

"God…." She began, peeling back the paper and saw a brown box inside. "Please make Terrence complete in you."

She opened the box. "Give him peace, security, and acceptance by you…" Delicate pink tissue paper surrounded and hid. "Free him from any imprisonment spirit that wants him to forget who he is in Christ…." She pulled the tissue paper apart and dropped them to the floor. "Help him to remember gifts that are given to him in Jesus."

Filled with anticipation, she finally revealed its contents, a photo album resting inside. She skipped through its pages and noticed pictures of all kinds. Her smile had now dispersed and she was captivated by his gift. She turned the page and there was a picture. The picture was one of her standing on her toes, frozen in a routine that she performed at church some eight months ago. She turned the leaves and there was a picture of Terrence, with his jaws filled with marshmallows, and he too was frozen in time as he gallivanted with the church sisters at a local restaurant. It wasn't until she was done turning the last page of the album that she noticed the warm liquid spilling out of her eyes and down her face.

As she breathed in, she finally came to understand the true meaning of *gift*.

And truly it was a phenomenal feeling—love wrapped in warm and precious memories and sealed with a selfless gesture. Madison didn't know exactly how to feel or what would become of this gift. Would she keep it and remember all of the special times or pack it away and try to forget the pain of not having *him* to herself? The answer wasn't easy and the stakes were much too high.

Yet, she looked around her and kept up pretenses well.

"What a lovely gift," someone said.

"There's nothing better than pictures to keep memories alive," she heard a male voice say.

And that was the problem—keeping the memories alive wasn't necessarily the right thing to do. But she smiled and answered politely, not even remembering what she said. It was almost like having an out of body experience and she knew that her spirit was in the presence of God. Suddenly, she was surrounded by peace and none of the confusion she dealt with previously. Madison closed her eyes and let the warmth run through her body, nothing but peace and love.

Then someone tapped her on the shoulder and Madison snapped out of her trance-like state. Everyone was staring at her as though they'd asked her a question and were waiting for an answer. So she did the only thing she could think of- distract them.

"Merry Christmas, everyone. I'm so happy to be sharing this holiday season with all of you," Madison said. "I know we must all have had such exciting plans in the past but this time we'll spend together."

And that was what did it; her comment started a conversation about the holidays and took all of the attention away from her and her gift. She sighed as she inched away from the crowd. *That was close.*

26 December 2010
Dear Babe,

As I sat in Tango 3, watching the ships and water waves move, I saw one of the dogs. It's the tan adult dog which looks healthy but unknown of the sex. Sergeant Jackson came by to check the generators and played with the dog for about 15m. The dog chased the ball while wagging its tail with energy and joy. It got a little thirsty and drank from his "water bowl" a soldier had made from the carryout trays. I would later make a "food bowl" from Cook's and I's lunch chow.

But when the sergeant left, the dog seemed sad as he dragged his body to the sand, snuggled up and fell on its side. I thought it collapsed and died of a broken heart. One of the Kuwait soldiers came by and threw something at the dog, and it ran. But the dog saw the group of Kuwaitis get near and it stood up defensively (preparing to run, hide, or defend itself.) Kuwaitis hate dogs and are known for beating them. So I thought, how did this dog survive? Perhaps, the same way I survived.

We knew of evil plots against our lives even as children, but we knew GOD better (Matthew 26:4).

GOD has a plan for us and it includes prosperity, giving hope, and a future. Even the events that seemed hopeless and cause us harm have to work for our best interest. When Joseph confronted his brothers after selling him into slavery, he said "You intended to harm me, but GOD intended it for good."

So now I try to remember that and not have my heart troubled about what people have done to me. I know no weapon formed against us will prosper. So when weapons appear in our lives, we can believe there is a spiritual significance because we do not fight against flesh. I've learned to ask the Father "What is the purpose?" (Romans 8:28).

Sometimes He answers suddenly and other times you wait. Perhaps, one purpose is we are forced to look to GOD and solely depend on him. GOD is jealous and we should always place him first. Taking things out of order can cause problems. Problems can't happen without GOD's permission because he is in control of your lives. So that should comfort us to know that we will continue and survive through life's problems.

So, Lord, I pray that you continue to teach us how to solely depend on you. Let us be like Paul and have such a close relationship with you that we aren't aware we have problems.

Let us be teachable and give us wisdom beyond our years to trust you completely no matter how things seem to appear on earth. We know you're doing it in the spirit. So fill us with excitement and prepare us to receive a great expectation, an overflow, and miracles. I'm calling upon the spirit of suddenly Lord move, rearrange, restore us like never before to receive for your glory Jesus' Name Amen.

The fresh sea breeze tickled Madison's face. It wrestled with her unkempt hair and the scent of salt, seaweed and sand filled her lungs. She noticed the white ripened clouds hovering over the dock; drifting, slowly towards the shore, she instantly fell into a meditative trance of how incredibly amazing God's greatness was portrayed through the elements. She closed her eyes and inhaled deeply. A breath of fresh air filtered its way through her nostrils. She listened to the waves rise and crash against the rocks, combusting into tiny crystals before reuniting with the sea. She imagined how the waves swam up to shore unto the sand, tempting and taunting it before slithering away. The sound of the ships roaring woke her up from her meditation and as she sat in Tango 3, she watched the ships pass by.

One of the dogs scampered up onto the beach; it scurried around in and out of empty containers, looking for scraps of food. It was a tan adult dog that looked healthy and Madison was unsure of its gender. Sergeant Jackson came by to check the generators.

"Corporal," he greeted her.

"Good afternoon sergeant," she responded, followed by a salute.

Sergeant Jackson whistled the dog over to him and immediately the two of them erupted into play. The hound jumped up on its hind legs and pressed its paws against the man, licking his face and wagging its tail. Sergeant pulled the ball he was carrying out of his pocket and the thrilled dog pranced about in excitement.

Madison watched intently, amused by the antics. He threw the ball, or so he made it appear and the dog went after the imaginary toy. The sergeant began to laugh again when the animal returned empty handed and disappointed. Finally, he let go of the ball, throwing it across the beach. The dog sped after it and retrieved the ball from the rubbles it was caught in.

The two played for almost fifteen minutes and soon they both grew weary. The dog drank from the makeshift bowl a soldier had created out of carryout trays and Sergeant Jackson massaged the muscles in his arm. Madison thought about making a food bowl for him from the lunch chow. Soon the Sergeant left the hound, and it desolately dragged its self across the sand, snuggled up and fell on its side. Madison thought it had died of a broken heart until one of the Kuwait soldiers came by.

His bald head glistened when the sun that peaked through the clouds struck it. He was a short man, with a scar splitting the top of his right brow. He scraped up some sand in his fist and threw it at the poor creature.

"Get outta here, you mangy mutt!" he retorted at the animal. The Kuwait soldiers detested dogs and Madison scoffed at his behavior. It made her wonder how it had survived all this time.

Perhaps, it survived the same way I did.

The dog ran when it was suddenly greeted by a group of Kuwaitis; they approached the animal and it did not retreat. It stood defensively, preparing to run, hide or defend itself.

Madison soon thought of the different obstacles, the different trials, heartaches and crosses that this life, this world…the devil was always creating. She thought about the heartbreak she experienced not so long ago and how she struggled to overcome that trial. And it had almost killed her as she lie in bed each day, crying and screaming, calling out to God, reasoning and questioning, wondering why.

It had been the worst time of her life and she had no intentions of ever repeating it. Every time the pain subsided, she'd told herself she would never love again, never trust again, but something inside her wouldn't let her give up. Yet, God pulled her through. He allowed her to see that no matter what circumstances may arise, she would always make it through, whole, renewed and loved by God. She wondered if she would ever be loved by Terrence just the same.

27 December 2010
Dear Babe,

A few days ago, we celebrated the birth of Jesus and how he died for our sins. As I did my prayer research, I was reminded of what Jesus' resurrection really meant…with GOD nothing is impossible (Luke 1:37). When Gabriel told Mary what GOD was going to do it seemed logically impossible. A virgin can not give birth to a child. But his thoughts and ways are not like ours. When GOD speaks, it becomes the truth and he is not a man that can lie. We can truly believe he can do the impossible.

GOD waits for you to believe the impossible then once you do then it done. When he speaks his plans, everything I already in place, he simply ask you to believe. Once you place your trust in him, great blessing will be experienced. I will be blessed because those things GOD spoke to me I believe (Luke 1:45).

I believe there are miracles waiting for us babe to believe because he is the same yesterday, today, and forever. So think of all the impossible things he did then. This why I couldn't give up because we are a miracle.

28 Dec 2010
Dear Babe,

Remember GOD is your strength, so rely on him and you will be great. Have a great day at work!

Before Madison could stop them, the memories came rushing back to her. They were once cautiously navigating the minefield of love and relationships like pros. Madison was over the dance program at the church they shared in the city. Terrence was one of the few men in the troop and was awed by Madison's talent the first time he saw her move by the Spirit. Her gracefulness and strength made it impossible to take his eyes off of her. She was older than him and she had seen young men approach her often with cloaked lust, but there was something different about Terrence. He seemed to have a spiritual maturity that intrigued her. Their friendship grew and Terrence soon found himself under Madison's spell. While Madison tried time after time to keep the relationship platonic, she found herself attracted to the young man. His ability to, quite literally, hold her and lift her up in perfect balance and not waiver was too much for her to ignore. Before long she found herself asking him to be her partner as they danced to the inspirational and melodramatic gospel-tinged songs. A passion for music and ministry was what they had most in common. Choirs roared while they moved arms, legs, necks, torsos, and feet to give honor to God, especially for filling their lives with one another.

Madison blushed whenever he touched her, which he did quite often; it was a routine they both enjoyed very much. As they both danced with a celestial intimacy, the spirit guided them across the stage. This wonderful, much older woman, glided gracefully, so much more graceful than any twenty-two-year-old, yet she was twice that age.

Every day they spent together seemed better than the day before as Madison believed she had finally found her soulmate, the one she could share her whole heart with. And Terrence understood her, the good and the bad, even all of her hidden issues; he'd spotted them and called them out from the beginning. And that kind of prophetic gifting she found amazing; he was everything she'd ever wanted in a man but once thought she could never have.

"You are so beautiful; there should be more of you," she whispered under an embarrassed breath as they walked home, holding hands. This was the custom; Terrence walked her home, dreading having to leave her at her door step.

"What would we call him?" he asked.

Madison looked at him curiously. " What would we call who? What do you mean?"

"The only way to make another me is for us to have a son together. So what would we call him?" Terrence grinned, never taking his eyes off of her.

She was taken aback and overwhelmed with an unfamiliar warmness. The thought of carrying his child made her feel maternal and content. His words sent a tingling feeling all throughout her body, and she giggled like a schoolgirl. He had such an affect on her that Madison wondered if he had done that on purpose.

"Oh, I don't know... I'd have to give a name some thought." Madison paused and there was an unbearable silence.

"How about Jeremiah?" they both said, simultaneously and then suddenly erupting in a hearty laugh, they groveled in the all too coincidental occurrence as though the epiphany was bestowed by God himself.

"How did you know?" Madison asked.

Terrence chuckled and took her in his arms. "No, how did you know?"

"So I guess we'll have a son..."

"And we'll call him Jeremiah," Terrence said.

"I can't wait," Madison said, looking up at him.

"Perhaps, we don't have to." Terrence moved in for a kiss.

"No, you'd better go before we get ourselves into trouble tonight," she said.

"You're right." Terrence backed away and put his hands behind his back." Temptation is great."

Madison shook her finger at him. "But greater is He who is in you than he who is in the world..."

They had meant everything to each other before the night Terrence forgot who he was in Christ and found himself consumed with lust. And lust had been the one thing that destroyed their relationship.

Madison felt her eyes cloud over again as her thoughts returned to the present. It made her sad to know that just two years earlier she and Terrence were in love and he had wanted her to carry his son, Jeremiah. The irony of it was beyond painful. Who knew he would have that son with someone else?

Madison saw Terrence wince in pain and she also saw a few drops of blood on the rock beside him.

Transmission from her dust covered radio suddenly buzzed and squeaked. "Special Evans Come in! Specialist Evans, please come in!"

The proving ground was intense; it opened a lot of doors and provided the perfect space for self-evaluation and the perfect opportunity to become not only physically but emotionally and spiritually stable.And she was grateful for this opportunity, knowing that it may never come again.

"How do you manage to get hit on the training ground, Private?" Specialist Evans screamed at them through the muffled radio.

"It...it was a stray bullet sir...came out of nowhere" Madison responded, pressing down hard on Terrence's open wound.

"You and your platoon pack it up and move out!"

Madison spat out, "Yes sir!"

"Guys, pack it up we are heading back to base!" Madison instructed, not giving it a second thought. It was the life of military personnel, giving and taking orders. She knew how to do both very well, almost too well. Sometimes she wondered if she could do anything other than that.

"What! One guy gets accidentally shot and the whole team gotta take the hit," one man protested.

"You heard the man!" Another responded, taking with him Terrance's bag and rifle.

Madison struggled to stand with Terrance and grasping onto her, he threw his arm around her shoulder.She wrapped one hand around his waist and the other she used to hold her rifle and bag. She pulled the rusty lime green and brown water bottle from her bag and put it to Terrence's mouth.

"Here drink," she ordered

He gulped it down, spilling some. Madison cradled Terrance and prayed a silent prayer to God for strength so she could bring them both safely back to the base.

"Madison, I never meant to-" Terrence started.

Madison interrupted him by putting her finger to his lips. "Shhh. I know," she said, quietly.

She knew that he wanted to apologize again, but it wasn't necessary; he had done so time and time again and it had never solved anything. It only left her feeling empty as usual. There was nothing that could be done to turn back the hands of time, to erase the mistake that Had grown into a barrier. There was nothing that could be done about the covenant that he had with his wife and the child that came from that union, although the child had come first. So much had been left unsaid, yet there was never any point in bringing up the past. Doing so would only bring them both back to a place they could no longer enjoy. Yes, it was over and the words, like the feelings, were best left behind.

29 Dec2010
Dear Babe,

> *Dreams can be interpreted in many ways, but surely we know what that dream meant. Surely we want GOD's Will for our lives. We need to be led by the Holy Spirit so we can have a renewed mind, good things are proven to us, acceptable, perfect, and GOD's Will.*
>
> *Lately, I've been having nightmares but I think it's the different spirits here in Kuwait. But you delivered us and keep us safe. So, Lord, I pray for peaceful sleep for us all. That our dreams are guided by sending your angels encamped around us. Angels excel in strength, do your word, heed your voice and you give angels charge over us to keep us in all ways. So I bring every thought, imagination, and dream into captivity and obedience of Jesus Christ. Even as we sleep, you reveal your purpose and plan for our lives.*
> *Psalm 92:11*
> *Psalm 103:20*

The first sense that regained consciousness after the explosion was the sense of smell and the scent of death which lingered in the air. Death smelled of fresh blood and gunpowder, which was a smell that never grows on you. It was a stinking, repulsive, sickening odor. Soon she could hear the trotting of boots, the explosions and the Ratt Tata of gunfire, the ear-splitting screams of falling soldiers and for a moment she thought she could hear the grim reaper's whisper. It seemed to be orchestrating his squad of farmers who would eventually till the earth and garnish the soil with the bodies of her comrades.

Then he would do what he did best which was to reap. Later the sense of sight seeped in and she struggled to lift her heavy eyelids. With smoke clouding her vision and debris threatening to blind her, she moved her gaze around and soon the smells and noises made sense. Lifeless, limbless bodies lie stretched out next to her, men curled up, behind boulders seeking refuge, groaning and moaning in pain. She could not move, that was the only sense that lingered, a temporary paralysis glued her to the hard dirt ground. However, a familiar cough and groan drew her attention.

To her bottom right, outstretched on the rubble pavement still clutching his weapon. Specialist Evans knew she could delay no longer and it wasn't until now that she realized how much she took for granted, how little she acknowledged the senses God bestowed her with; now she needed them more than ever. Her body was in shock, wanting desperately to move, and to feel but the forces prevented her from doing so. Again she heard him cry out in pain and this sent life thrusting inside of her. She was overwhelmed and overcome by a sudden burst of energy, a new found vigor. It was Terrence and he needed her; she felt that it was God directing her to him.

Suddenly, Madison moved her body into an upright position, in one slow motion. She remembered the first time Terrence was wounded; they were on the training ground, she dropped her rifle at the sound of the explosion and it went off, hitting Terrence straight in the leg. It was an accident and they called it "a stray bullet." But then, then she would have rushed to his aid, knowing very well that help was not far off. Then, they would have laughed it off nervously and she would have apologized a thousand times. Then He would be fixed up and up and running in no time. But now, she knew help was nowhere near them. She knew that this was no accident; she knew that neither of them would laugh and as she crawled to him, with tears welled up in her eyes. *Surely it's too good to be true* Terrence had escaped death once before and she would make sure he would do it again....

45

She skidded to his side, panting desperately, calling his name. And he responded to her by grabbing onto her hand.

She could not shake the feeling, the feeling of loss and desperation. He has been hit twice! "Maybe I'll lose him; maybe it's too good to be true…. Maybe…," she whispered to herself as her thought was interrupted by a rain of gunfire. She rolled on top of him. The two embraced and whispered a silent prayer…

"WE…WE'VE GOT TO GET C…COVER!!" Terrence bellowed in a broken husky puff. Specialist Evans counted every slow heaving motion of his chest; she had to check his wound, but there was not much she could do as it was. The two were in the eye of the storm and as she begged God to deliver them suddenly, the rain ceased.

30 Dec 2010
Dear Babe,

I got on the phone today and spoke with a friend who went on and on complaining. She mentioned giving up on her potential boyfriend, worrying about bills, finding a house, divorce, etc. And before I knew it, my joyous self felt drained. I am not saying she's a bad person, but perhaps I should limit myself speaking to her and others. Our relationships do influence us through good our bad influence. Terrence, I pray GOD gives us discernment to separate ourselves from anyone who will not be good influence (I Cor 5:13).

Send godly male friends to you and godly female friends to me who we can openly share our hearts with. May our friends be trustworthy and speak truth into our lives and not just say what we want to hear. (Proverbs 28:32). Let us appreciate our friends but make each other "best friends" inspire us Lord to use open communication and acceptance with each other. Allow your love to cover us that we won't carry grudges against each other in our hearts. Lord, let us continue to walk in forgiveness and love each other because we will all stand before judgment

(Romans 14:10). Enable us to love our enemies and do good to those who hate us (Matthew 5:44). Show us what it means to be a true friend like you are a friend to us. I pray Terrence counts me as his best friend and our friendship will continue to grow in Jesus' Name Amen.

Specialist Evans used her right hand to slide the camouflage jacket off of his body. He was hit and she had to see how bad the damage was. As she removed layers upon layers of clothing from his limp muscular physique, she thought of all the times she had done this before, but never had it been life or death. Never had it been more than moments of pure pleasure.

Terrence Billings was outstretched on the rubble pavement still clutching his weapon. Madison whose uniform read Specialist Evans, took it from his grip and screamed, "Terrence, hang on I'm here now!!"

He looked into her deep mahogany brown eyes as they began to water and said, "It's no use. I'm dead weight to you."

She drew on an air of desperation and closed the now open fabric of his uniform like a curtain. She laid beside him to lay low because of the falling debris from the blast. She suddenly remembered all the times she had lain beside him, in the coziness of the apartment they had once shared. *God, forgive us for living in sin.*

"Dead weight to me? No, no, you are wrong. You are everything to me! It's not too late; it'll never be too late!" she yelled in her mind as determination racked her thoughts.

Years, like weeds, had sprouted between them. He was married now with a child and not

in that order. Everything had turned against her and had gone wrong. Everything had been stolen from her, the man she loved, the child she dreamed of carrying and her hope for the future; and she was empty.

Lord, please fill me again.

She plotted her next move to get them under cover. As she sucked in air, sand coated her nose and lips. Her own weapon was heavy against her ribs. She asked God to get them to safety, and if He did, then she would surely have to ask Him about the strange turn of events that had led them to this moment. She couldn't understand it at all. Why they had been thrown together again? Why she was continually tormented by a man who could never be hers? But for the moment, she had to put it all out of her mind and persevere; she had to be strong for the both of them.

She saw a cave fifty feet away. She held her breath, grabbed her fellow soldier under the arm, and used her own body weight to allow him to stand. She said nothing as she began galloping toward the cave. She had underestimated her speed and within seconds found herself dropping to her knees with Terrence as they reached it safely.

"A head's up would've been nice," Terrence coughed out instead of a more appropriate thank you.

She smiled nervously and breathed an uneasy response, "I…did not think you needed to be in on the plan seeing you're wounded and I'm not, Drill Sergeant Billings."

He was no drill sergeant, but she thought he did a pretty good impression of theirs, especially in that instance. Secretly, she admired him. Whether he knew it or not, he'd always been her hero.

"That blast was a bitch!" Terrence announced the obvious, shaking his head, slightly. "This is more real than anything we ever did in basic," Madison commented. "But

I sure am glad we had the training."

"I don't know how this happened. The whole camp is secured," he said.

"Was secure," she corrected.

Terrence spoke slowly and methodically. "I guess things aren't always a sure thing."

She wondered if he was eluding to their relationship or if his words about the incident were just coincidentally fitting.

"I guess they aren't," she agreed. "Terrence, what did you see when the blast happened?"

"Huh?"

"Like…what was going through your mind?" she pressed on, hoping with all her heart that she was on his mind.

"Honestly... my son," was his candid response.

Madison had suspected that he would answer that way but still she was grateful that he hadn't mentioned his wife, Monique.

"I thought about his smile and his laugh. I thought about the way he stretches his arms out when he sees me. I thought of his face when I tickle his feet...."

He went on and Madison relaxed for a moment, listening to his recount of what seemed to be a beautiful yet tragic experience. His story soon became sad and melancholic and Madison could listen no more. She turned her head away, masking a tear. She could not listen to him carry on about a son that was not hers, not theirs, a son she thought she was destined to bear for him.

"His silly antics...Madison, are you alright?" he called her, noticing her sudden withdrawal.

"Yeah," she lied, then in a deep, shaky breath, she said, "We...we should get your wound patched up."

Didn't he realize how much he had hurt me? How could he not know how hollow I feel on the inside? Did he really think that love could be turned off at a moment's notice without carrying the residue of what was before? Madison didn't know the answer to any of her questions and she seriously doubted that she would ever know. But she knew that the love of God was greater than anything she had ever felt for Terrence and greater than anything that he had ever felt for her. He would have to clean up the mess that was left behind because He was the only one who could.

31 Dec 2010
Dear Babe,

I love GOD so much....I prayed the other night for spending time with you and I got an entire day! But loving Him is not enough, but I want to glorify him on earth by completing the last detail of my assignment (s) (John 17:4). The more time I am with you, the move I know you are my assignment. An assignment which is almost complete. I'm excited because once something ends another thing is born. It is GOD who has given us new lives that we should spend these lives helping others (Ephesians 2:10).

So, Babe, I am so proud that GOD choose you as one of my assignments win which I am able to help. Terrance, I pray that GOD continues to bless us, keeping our focus on him and acknowledging him everything we do. Father, I adore you for giving Terrence and me life on this earth and giving us assignments. Let us glorify you in each endowed and trust you for the impartation you have already given us to be successful in each of them and to please you.

In the middle of her thoughts, she heard the distinctive voice of Sergeant Christopher Paniagua and Madison was grateful he had realized she was missing. Chris was a true soldier in every sense of the word. She still remembered the day he came to the medic bay to check on her after stress fractures got her held back in basic.

She jumped off of the table when he entered the room. There she was with her fatigues rolled high to her thigh on one leg. He wasn't threatening, even though he stood six-foot-four in combat boots. He looked like Dewayne "the Rock" Johnson, on a good day. His straight white teeth and neat perfectly cropped curls were evidence he was no regular Army jock. He never took off that silver cross and openly prayed before his meals. His bi-racial heritage made him popular with all the *fellas* because his looks were racially ambiguous. This was also an asset in foreign affairs.

Chris spoke four languages, including the one his grandfather had taught him as a boy when he visited in the summers–Curacao. He had learned Dutch, Spanish, English and even Creole. That day at the medics, his eyes were so soft and caring.

But today Madison noticed he fumbled over his words when he saw her exposed dancer's leg.

"Why did you join up?" he asked, looking as if he was concentrating hard on not looking at her leg. "I've been dying to ask you that for so long."

Madison tried to cover her leg but smiled at the consistency of human nature. "God told me to."

As she spoke, she realized he cringed as if her words were like fire in his soul, but she continued, "I was in a place in my life where I kept stumbling. I wasn't progressing, I wasn't growing. I was alone in the studio and I was rehearsing to a song called 'Battle Cry.' It was then that I had the revelation. I was already at war within and decided my training to be a true fighter would need to be both physical and spiritual. So, here I am."

It was the story she once told to everyone when her faith was new and fiery; it was her own personal testimony and no one and nothing could take it from her. Ironically, Chris was never good with words, although he possessed the ability to speak so many languages.

It was obvious when he blurted, "Really? The rest of the platoon thought it was to escape."

This irritated Madison.

"Escape what?" she asked sharply, forgetting she was only a curtain away from being alone with Sergeant Paniagua, an Army no-no in basic, and while on duty at that. "Escape heart-ache."

"Escape heartache," he repeated as if he was unsure if Madison had heard him, but she had. Loud and clear. Her guard went up and she felt her body turn rigid. How much did he know? Had Terrence told him about the two of them? *How dare he.* Her ankle began to throb and the pain must've been apparent on her face because he asked her if she was ok. She quickly got her bearings.

"Escape heartache? No...that's not the sort of thing you can run away from. It can be troublesome and never far away," she answered, confidently, although she was a wreck on the inside.

She had worked too hard to attain her position and she refused to lose his respect because of her own personal weakness. She would bind her weak heart if she had to, but she would never allow it to be betrayed again. She would go into any and all relationships with her eyes wide open, asking for nothing, giving nothing, and expecting nothing in return. *I'll have total control.* Then she remembered her personal relationship with God and knew that, He, alone, had control.

In any case, she stood boldly staring at him while he fidgeted nervously, looking as if her words had found a tiny pore and dug their way into him. He was silent for a moment until a medic pulled back the curtain that separated them.

"Sergeant, now you know this place is off limits…even for you," she added hastily.

The bleak barracks were all a faded pale blue: the walls, the bed covers, the steel that the bunks were made of, even the cement floors. The entire room looked as if it was underwater. Madison spent ten hours in the medics and was exhausted. She had undergone head trauma tests for hours before finally being released. She had stayed waiting, however, until she received news that Billings' surgery had been a success.

He received sixteen stitches for a slice that was only two inches from his right kidney. He had to be the luckiest person she knew…well other than herself. She found her bunk, just big enough to accommodate her 5'7, 130-pound frame and laid down on top of the wool Army- issued blankets. The rubble finally escaped her curly strands and made a new home on her pillow case. She was asleep within moments.

Specialist Maria Suarez woke her with a jolt.

"Evans, they might be giving you a purple heart! Man, you saved Billings…said you pulled into a cave and kept him alive and warm for four hours after the explosion. They said if it weren't for you, he would be dead. You're a hero, man!"

Madison had to decipher Maria Suarez' Spanish-tinged words before she completely understood. "W-what? They don't give out Purple Hearts for that. It wasn't even real combat, Maria."

Madison knew that Special Suarez hated being called Maria. Her thick Puerto Rican hair was always wound tightly in a bun. She never wore makeup and yet her large brown eyes came equipped with eyelashes that required no mascara at all, as did her pouty, naturally crimson lips, which she drew up in a sneer.

"Fine! I'll take the Purple Heart then…"

She heard her murmur, "Stupid," as she hopped up on her own bunk two rows over.

1 Jan 2010
Dear Babe,

Since this is the first day of the year, I thought about the significance of the number one. GOD said I am the alpha and omega the beginning and the end which is and which was, which is to come the Almighty. GOD is the first and the last (Rev 1:11). I still can not imagine that there was nothing, but only GOD here in this spiritual realm. Before GOD, there was nothing and before nothing GOD always existed. Can you imagine just GOD existing forever! GOD began creating things perhaps because he was lonely or bored. The waters under heaven be gathered together unto one place, and let the dry land appear and it was so (Genesis 1:9). And at one point, the entire earth was unified with one language (Genesis 11:1). Can you imagine no confusion and the greatest communication of all?

It is proven again and again how GOD loves this number one. The number one is powerful and up the flesh (Genesis 2:21). There is definitely a connection about GOD making Eve out of Adam from one rib and symbolizing man/wife becoming one (Genesis 2:24). Perhaps, because GOD is one and he uses that to illustrate his meaning throughout eternity. So let's celebrate this first day of the year together as one.

Lord, thank you for giving Terrence and I this opportunity to share this first day of the year together. Unify us as you did Adam and Eve and let us be an example how a true union of marriage should be like in Jesus' Name Amen

The flame from the lonesome candle illuminated the dark space, and it danced as the wind from the slightly cracked window taunted it. The dimly lit room was cozy and Madison shuffled uneasily in the large chair. She shifted her eyes around the small apartment, eating up all the fine details of his modern furniture. Their silhouettes were graceful and though most of the pieces were overcast by shadows, she could tell they were of fine taste. A picture hung on the wall and it was slightly crooked. This annoyed Madison and she rose and approached the flawed frame. She struggled to straighten the stubborn art.

"It won't fix. Believe me, I've tried."

Terrence returned to the room with two more candles in hand. Madison withdrew and sighed with defeat. She stood back and stared at the slanted picture, then shook her head in disgust before turning to take one of the candles from him.

"What a night for the powers to be out, huh?" she said as she dripped hot wax onto a metal saucer. Terrance shrugged and again he disappeared into the darkness of the other room. She stuck the candle to the hot wax and waited for it to dry. The candle now had a base to stand on. She returned to her seat and waited anxiously for her host to return. In the shadowy distance of the room, on a small table in the corner, Madison caught a glimpse of pamphlets, informative brochures and 'how to' guides.

There was a soldier decorated in camouflage, saluting on the front of each leaflet. Madison was intrigued and reached for the pile. At first she picked up the very one on top and it read in bold Italicized letters, *"The soldier is the Army. No army is better than its soldiers. The Soldier is also a citizen and the highest obligation and privilege of citizenship is that of bearing arms for one's country."*

She scowled and picked up the second one, which read, *"Out of every one hundred men, ten shouldn't even be there, eighty are just targets, nine are the real fighters, and we are lucky to have them, for they make the battle. Ah, but the one—one is a warrior, and he will bring the others back."*

For some odd reason, Madison's mind wandered.

What an awful day that was, the day she found out that she had been betrayed, the day she lost everything. She still remembered it like it was yesterday.

She was sitting in his apartment, or theirs, as she liked to refer to it since she'd unofficially moved in. As she saw a pile of papers that was out of place. Normally something like that would not have been unusual for her, but Terrence always kept everything immaculate. Seeing the scattered papers alarmed her, and she sighed as she picked up the whole pile, but something heavy fell to the ground. It looked like a pen on first glance. However, when she returned the papers slowly back to their place and picked it up, upon further investigation, she noticed that it was a test, white with two strips of lines going down it. Shaking, she held it in her hands and inspected it.

Terrence had slipped in behind her and stopped in his tracks. She could only hear his breathing and the tinkling of glasses.

"So…." Terrence held two glasses and a bottle of wine. He handed her one and she stretched out her hand to receive it, reluctantly. She looked at him blankly, watching as his gaze moved to the object in her left hand. The silence was stifling.

All the blood left his face; he was suddenly pale and looked sickly. He appeared as though he had seen a ghost. Madison was worried and raised her brows in concern.He finally released the distressed breath of air he was holding onto.

"What is this?" she asked, with tears forming in her eyes.

"I uh…it's…. a pregnancy test," he breathed.

"I know what *it* is," she said.

"But I mean what is it doing here? Why…do…do…you have it?" Madison stuttered.

Terrence avoided her eyes.

"Sit down…we need to talk," he beckoned

Pain was already rising up in Madison.

"I can talk just fine standing up. Why do you have a pregnancy test? And…" She looked at it scornfully, then tossed it at his feet. "And why has it been used!!??"

Terrence moved in closer to Madison, waving his hands and trying to calm her down. "I want you to please just listen."

Madison blinked away the tears. "And why wouldn't I listen? Don't I always listen? Why would this be different?"

Terrence swallowed hard. "Well, because I don't want you to be upset and not allow me to finish what I have to say."

"And why would I be so upset? What have you got to tell me." Madison was already preparing herself for the blow.

Terrence started, "Something happened between my ex-girlfriend and me around Christmastime...."

Madison squinted her eyes. "Monique?"

"Yes...Monique."

"And by *something* I am assuming you...." She choked on a tear. "You mean you had sex with her?"

Terrence dropped his head in shame and answered, "Yes."

Madison began to shake her head slowly, as she imagined what he was about to say. "And she's...pregnant?"

"Yes," he confirmed. "But it was all a mistake and I..."

"A mistake? You mean like an error in judgment? No, this is more than just a mistake; it's a catastrophe."

Madison felt as though the floor slipped away from beneath her. She drew on a cold air, one that stifled her, and she sank almost effortlessly into the sofa.

Terrance poured a glass of wine and handed it to her. "Here please, drink something...I...and I'll explain."

"Explain? You really think I want you to explain? After all we've meant to each other, there is nothing that you could possibly say that could make it right so no I don't want you to explain."

Madison grabbed the glass of wine from his hand and threw it against the wall, watching it splatter into pieces.

"Madison, I'm sorry. I didn't..." Terrence pleaded.

"You didn't what, Terrence? You didn't know that a woman could get pregnant if you have sex with her? You didn't know that you were a man and, therefore, vulnerable to the charms of your ex-girlfriend? Or did you not know that she would actually get pregnant and therefore caught? How many times have you done this before?"

Terrence kneeled down in front of her. "None, I swear. There was only this one time and I.."

"Nevermind; it doesn't even matter. I should've known better, but I trusted you. I thought that you were different than the other men I've been involved with in the past. And I thought that what we had together was special. But that was my mistake."

Madison pulled herself up from the sofa and started to walk towards the door. Terrence took her by the hand. "But please listen…"

Madison jerked her hand away from his.

"I don't care what you have to say. One time or twenty times; it's all the same. You're a liar and a cheat," Madison shouted.

"Please calm down. The neighbors…"

"Do you think I care about the neighbors. You've gotten someone else pregnant and you're only concerned about how loud I am. You don't want them to know about your mistake."

Madison bent her body and began to whisper. "Well, pardon my outbursts; let me excuse myself from your apartment and then it will be quiet again."

Madison grabbed her bag.

"I'll pick up the rest of my things another time."

"Please wait…"

"No…no I should go. Happy New Year to you, Terrance"

And with that she left.

It had been a devastating start to the new year—one that should've started with excitement and celebration had been tainted with the stench of lust and disillusionment. As she left his apartment building, she knew her life would never be the same again.

2 Jan 2011
Dear Babe,

Beginning a new season means that there will be change. I thought about my past and how I can improve this year. The question which popped into my head was "How did I fail?" I have failed so often (Romans 7: 14-25). I admit some my failures death with playing with sin (2 Cor 6:17). I thought I could control my flesh once I did leave GOD, but I was just believing the lie because I can't fight in my own strength (2 Cor 12: 9-10). I also realized I didn't pray as much as I should have which led to failures (I Thes 5:17). I know one plot of the enemy is to make you feel guilty which takes your walk with GOD further from him (John 12:35). But I acknowledge that I am too weak of character to make it on my own strength (2 Cor 12: 1-11)

Specialist Billings layed flat on his stomach, pressing hard against the tall grass. He, along with his other comrades, blended in quite well, or so they thought. Terrance flexed his fingers around his rifle and gripped it. A bead of sweat trickled down the side of his face. The scent of fresh wet grass was pungent and he inhaled deeply, slowly. The only thing the soldier could hear was his hushed breathing and the crickets chirping.

The night was glorious, the sky was clear and free from any dark clouds. The stars smiled down at them and the moon was colossal and pregnant, radiant as it rained its illumination across the field. The night's dew bathed them in a blanket of white as they lay still, like logs on the earth. This was it, this was war...war was silent but deadly.

The men (and women) waited patiently, quietly. Terrance heard a rustling not too far from him; he contracted his trigger finger and slowed his breath. The high grass was being trampled, massacred! Dozens of armed men approached. Trotting through the field, they whispered hushed instructions in a thick foreign accent. Surely, they could attack and possibly defeat the approaching men, but they knew they were not alone. Just below them; at the bottom of the cliff hundreds of other men awaited them.

There was a thump on his arm, which sent a terrifying shockwave rushing through his body. It was Sergeant Paniagua and he was withdrawing. Specialist Billings was too busy focusing on the approaching enemies to notice when the corporal gave the order. He watched him slither below him, when he raised a finger, pointed it at Specialist Billings and then indicated with his thumb to retreat. Terrence nodded understanding.

Just as he was about to move, a deadly viper glided up his elbow and onto his face. He stiffened his body and let the lethal creature caress the left side of his face. It slithered, smelling his cheeks with its tongue; the boots that trampled the grass were upon him. The others were dispersed across the field, but one soldier lingered. The toe of his boot was a rusty lime green, inches away from his face, and it was grimy with mud and grass stuck to it. Beads of sweat threatened to blind him; his cheeks were hot, and his breathing slowed down so much that it seemed he had stopped altogether. Terrance was sure the thumping of his heart would have given away his position; it tumbled and tossed within his chest, pounding and banging in heavy, fast unorganized tumults.

The poisonous snake that crawled betwixt and around him threatened him and taunted him. If even a single drop of its venom got inside of him, it would cripple him with pain; yet, it was the least of his concern.

His gaze followed the carefree slitherer, closing his eyes as places he didn't even expect to have sweat glands, seeped and leaked with the salty water. As he opened his eyes, he looked dead on into the barrel of a cold metallic tool. He felt his bowels move. Stiffened by an abrupt burst of panic, Specialist Billings gripped his rifle. 'It's kill or be killed' and just as he was about to attempt an attack, the soldier used the rifle to slap the viper away. There was a horrific pause and the soldier retreated.

Specialist Billings gathered his nerves and soon made his way to safety, and then finally caught up with his unit. Billings struggled to wrap his head around what just took place. It didn't make sense to him. Why was he spared? Why he was not killed or captured? He removed the crumpled photo he had hidden away in his vest; his son smiled back up at him. He turned the picture around and in smeared ink, he read, "In the valley of the shadow of death, I will fear no evil for thou art with me…"

3 Jan 2011
Dear Babe,
    I feel the change has begun (we are in our next season). Everything was stolen, given away, or lost was restored to us. I am so excited that I sold two t-shirts, but mostly excited because it came from the Lord so I know it will be successful. The word says, and he shall be like a tree planted by the rivers of water, that brings forth his fruit in his season; his leaf also shall not wither; and whatsoever he doeth shall prosper. (Psalms 1:1-3 KJV)

….the purpose of today's ceremony is to recognize the commitment of the men and women you see standing in formation before you today, who have chosen to serve their country as soldiers. This review is the last official formation of the training cycle. Not everyone successfully completes this difficult period of training but those in formation today represent discipline, motivated, physically fit soldiers, who exemplify the army's seven core values: Loyalty, duty, respect, selfless service, honor, integrity and personal courage. They're imbued with the warrior ethos and display the tenants of putting the mission first, never accepting defeat, never quitting and never leaving behind a fallen comrade. This is an important day and they can take great pride in their accomplishments. To the parents, families and friends of these soldiers we extend a very warm and sincere welcome. We are justifiably proud of them and equally honored that they have chosen to join our ranks…

No one slept that night because silent prayers became noise and whispers went on long into the night. Uniforms were so neatly pressed, starched and spotless, boots were polished and shined so much so that your reflection could be seen in them. Badges, buttons, and crests were pinned on, sewn in and tacked down. As they anxiously awaited the break of dawn, stifled laughter, and muffled bits of chitter chatter and the occasional sniffles and hushed sobs, all could be heard within the dorms where soldiers lay stretched out on their bunks.

Fond and tragic memories would be recollected. Congratulations and goodbyes would be exchanged. Confessions and secrets would be told that night. That night, the last night…the night where the glow of a firefly shone brighter than usual, where the number of stars hanging from the black blanket was more abundant than usual and where the full moon seemed fuller than usual.

The men and women were like children that morning, busy-bodies, hustling, and bustling. They were the first to arise. They beat the annoying horned alarm sound and were up and buzzing even before Drill Sergeant Wright could come in screaming "Rise and shine, maggots!" This was it for all who thought they would not have made it this far; all of the doubts all of the fears, all of the times they wanted to give up, throw in the towel, call it a day no longer mattered. They were now the very ones, who at the fall of dusk, would be graduated from the training ground as men and women prepared to fight and die for their country.

Terrance and Madison passed occasional coy glances at each other. They ate heartily that morning and took extra care in grooming themselves. Today they would be reunited with their families and friends. Many of the women and men from the Assemblies of the First Born Church would be present to celebrate Maddison's and Terrence's feat. Madison's brother, Paul, his wife Martha, their son and daughter, Pauline and Mark would be present. Her father had passed away, but her mother flew in from the Bahamas determined not to miss the occasion. Madison's smile widened and she paused in between lacing her shoes to give God thanks.

TERRENCE

errance reflected while he got a haircut, on how much basic combat training had pushed this recruit's mind and body to extraordinary limits. How it had given him a deeper respect for himself and those around him. *Now, the time has come to celebrate the efforts of me and my comrades and the strength we've gained.* This was the day that their families and friends would gather to watch them transition from citizens to soldiers. From civilians to warriors!'

4 Jan 2011
Dear Babe,

In I Corinthians 12, the Bible defines the different types of spiritual gifts. Those spiritual gifts include the following: wisdom, knowledge, faith, gift of healing, miraculous powers, prophecy, discernment (distinguishing between spirits), speaking in tongues and interpretation of tongues (I Corinthians 12:8-10). The Bible mentions additional spiritual gifts in I Corinthians 12:28-30: apostleship, teaching, helping others, and administration. Some of the spiritual gifts are mentioned in both passages. All are gifts from the Holy Spirit. I know everyone won't have the same gifts, but I don't think GOD would limit you and you can't have this gift unless he knows you would use it for another purpose or it's just not meant for you to have. I didn't even want the gifts I have now. As a child, I thought I was crazy because I saw spirits even at a young age. Later on once I got saved, I was finally able to understand a little, but it wasn't until adulthood I really accepted my gifts and understood its' purpose. I needed answers so I did research on prophetic and seeing spirits. I went to prophetic conferences and knowing your gifts in the spirit seminars, read books, and prayed. About ten years ago, I found out my aunt used to deal with witchcraft and she would babysit us as children. I was told my aunt would hear demons speak to her and tell her things. I always sensed this evil about her, but could not explain it. But my mom said I was always like that. She thinks even as a baby I would see spirits and I believe that because they are so innocent and free of sin then.

My dad is prophetic but has used it for bad as well. So I think it is a gift passed down from generation and I am one of the first to use the gift as GOD intended it for.

I've told anyone, I mean anyone about me going into traces. I use to do it all the time and thought I was crazy. I prayed many years to get freed from it and it hasn't happened lately so I figured it wasn't from GOD or perhaps I still can't handle the gift. But I am not sure. For example, I could be in the middle of doing something and I get a vision and get inside the vision. I know that sounds crazy, but it's true. Whatever that is happening in the vision I act like I'm there. But the enemy knew my gift and would try to trap me there in that spiritual realm.

Being prophetic I think is all tied into spiritual awareness. According to the Bible, while all spiritual gifts are from the Holy Spirit, not every spiritual gift is considered equal. In I Corinthians 12:31, the Bible encourages us to "eagerly desire the greater gifts."

Presumably, the greater gifts are those that are mentioned first, such as apostleship, prophecy, and teaching (I Corinthians 12:28). However, the Bible also explains in I Corinthians 12:12-26 that God's followers are all interconnected and that each spiritual gift has a role. All are important.

Jesus exhibited many of the spiritual gifts, such as the gifts of healing (Matthew 4:23), prophecy (Revelation 19:10), and performing miracles (Acts 2:22). According to the Bible, Jesus said that anyone with faith in him will do the same things that he did, including even greater things (John 14:12). This implies Jesus' authorization of spiritual gifts. Jesus' words were true for many of the apostles, including Paul (Acts 19:11) and Peter (Acts 3:1-10). The purpose of spiritual gifts is to benefit the body of Christ. According to the Bible, the Holy Spirit gives us spiritual gifts for the common good. (I Corinthians 12:7) God's people are to work together, using their spiritual gifts, to glorify God and to help one another.

So I pray Lord, that the spiritual gifts that you have given Terrence and I are given back to you. We use our spiritual gifts as you intended to for your glory. Let us not use our gifts for personal gain, but remember to allow your presence in everything we do. Jesus, I pray that even the gifts that are hidden are known right now to use, and we are able to use every gift to help others, and to develop the gifts we have now for your glory. In Jesus' Name, Amen.

It was a delightful feeling, a tummy tingling, heart pounding, wonderfully ecstatic feeling and each soldier could not contain their glee. Many were not afraid to shed some tears. Others held back, masking their sobs behind roaring belly laughs.

…This is the official start of the graduation ceremony, it is customary to raise at the call of attention marking the arrival of our guest speaker the president of the United States of America, Barrack Obama. After the official party has been announced and has arrived on the platform, please remain standing and render appropriate courtesies for honors to the President of the United States of America and to the national anthem of the United States of America. Uniformed members will salute, military veterans are encouraged to salute and civilians are encouraged to show the same courtesy to our nation, by removing their hats and placing their right hand over their hearts. We encourage you to join in the singing of our national anthem at its completion we ask that you remain standing. As a courtesy, please rise when the president completes his address to the soldiers before us today. At the conclusion of this ceremony, the soldiers before us will perform a drill, at its completion we ask that you join us in celebrating our soldiers with hearty cheers and vivacious rounds of applauds. We will then recess, here all may depart to be reunited with family and friends, we ask that you welcome them with open arms, admiration, praise and sincere fondness…

Almost as though their entrance was choreographed, the soldiers graced the crowd with their presence. One after the other, neatly groomed and polished with the finest of pish and posh marched in to the sound of the orchestra's serenade. Expressionless, or so it would appear at first glance, they stood almost like robots before being "ordered" to be seated. As ordained the afternoon proceed almost effortlessly if you don't consider the random outbursts of patrons and well-wishers screaming "YOU GO, JOHN!!!" "MAARRYY THAT'S MY GIRL!!" and the all too often 'Woohs' and 'Yays'. There was a lengthy prayer to start the proceeding, delivered by Sergeant Bullock; he was known for lengthy prayers. There was the singing of the national anthem and the presentations of awards and tokens to the awardees and special guests. Addresses, tributes and speeches were made And then finally there was the recess.

Like the mass, and in upholding the traditions, Madison and Terrence dispersed to greet the approaching crowd. With a hearty reception, Madison's brother, Paul scooped her up into his arms; she then hugged her sister-in-law and bent to cradle her niece and nephew. Madison removed her hat and her blazer, putting the hat onto her six-year-old niece's head and draping the blazer around her eight-year-old nephew's shoulders. She rose to look at her mother who she had not seen in almost four years. With her eyes pooled up with tears and her heart swelling inside her chest, her wide eyes drank up the fullness of the aging woman before her. Years skipped past them like book leaves and she could not recognize her own mother. She was old, fragile, and pale. It scared her, thrilled her, and confused her, all at once.

Her mother smiled up at her and they embraced, as she smothered her face with wet kisses, brushing away the tears that began to spill out of her wells.

"I'm so sorry Ma, I am so so sorry…Ma..ma Please forgive me…" she tightened her embrace.

"Uh! My child, my sweet flower, why are you apologizing? There is nothing to forgive, oh, Madison…let me be proud of you girl! There is nothing to forgive," and they cried and laughed.

Madison stood desperately scanning the crowd, twisting and turning, searching for Terrance. She could not find him, but her heart palpitated as she almost choked with anticipation and glee! Trying hard to resist the temptation to bellow his name, she was seconds away from bursting into a run, around the field to find him.

Suddenly, she turned and standing in front of her only a mere half yard away was Terrance, grinning an ear to ear grin. His mother and sister stood behind him immersed in conversation. She stood as he walked towards her, up to her, then passed her. Terrence was now behind her, hugging another woman, kissing and embracing someone who was not her. She turned to see him take a child from the woman and bury his face into his chest, tossing the lad into the air and receiving him with hugs and kisses.

The woman was obviously Monique, who stood by and watched Terrence play with Jeremiah, his son. The scene was utterly heartbreaking for Madison, but it was necessary to bring her back to reality—the new reality. There was no Madison and Terrence; there was only Monique and Terrence. It was a hard lesson, but she had to learn it and accept it, no matter how hard it was to swallow. The truth was often difficult to digest but what were her choices?

To go on pining away for a man who could never be hers? To defy God's commandments and promises by continuing to covet another woman's husband instead of waiting for her own blessing? But that was where the confusion had come in because she once believed that God had sent Terrence to her, for her. *Maybe I was wrong.*

5 Jan 2011
Dear Babe,

Thank you for keeping your word. I admit there is still something there when you say something, and you don't follow through with it for whatever reason. I know you're not perfect and things come up, but I'm still learning to trust you again. Therefore, if you fail, admit it and change. Because your word means everything to me. You're the only one here who understands me and who I can relate to. When you come through for me, it proves I can trust you and count on you. And whatever you do, whether in word or deed, do it all in the name of the Lord Jesus. (Colossians 3:17 NIV)

Terrence, I pray that you continue to speak truth in your heart (Psalm 15:1,2) and when you say something you mean it. But to remember your tongue is powerful and can bring life or death. Encourage others when they are down and pull on the strength of the Lord. Let him guide you in everything you do so he can get the glory out of it. I pray that I can totally trust you again and will not be hurt by you again. But we are made new creatures and old things are passed away. We can depend on each other for everything and always look to you, Lord, first.

Madison's smile melted, her heart collapsed and her throat constricted as tears stung her eyes. Her lashes fought effortlessly to blink them away, but it was futile. They spilled out of her face as if they had a mind of their own and soon she was choking on a world of emotions. Pain threatened to cripple her as her hands trembled and she could feel a hurt knotting within her stomach, a new found kind of pain, leaving her ill. The hand of agony wrapped its fingers around her heart....

"Ma!" she managed to call out, "Take...this...badge off of me!"

Her words were chopped and weak, and between sobs she declared," I don't…have use for it anymore! It's getting dark, too dark to see, and I feel like I'm knocking on heaven's door!"….

"Madison, don't say that! Just listen to my voice! Look at me, Mad; focus on me…. My voice!" Terrance hollered.

He held on to her for dear life, pressing hard into her wound. Blood seeped from her mouth and the crimson liquid stained her slender neck. He could see it in her large eyes that she wouldn't make it. He kissed away the ice cold tears that cascaded down her face. She was growing pale.

All of the men were dispersed at the base of the mountain, trying desperately to light up its peak with gun fire, in a futile effort to kill the men who threatened to kill them. Still, it was in vain, as one by one they went down, a shot to the head, a shot to the chest.

"Damn it! We are losing men like flies out here, Sarge!!!" Terrence yelled.

"Billings, round up your men! We need to get to the top of that hill!!"

So said, so done. Terrence and his squad poured in, perched behind boulders and trees they shot rounds after rounds.

"UGH!!!" Specialist Rector was hit,

"Shit! Let's move!"

Specialist Billings grabbed into the collar of Specialist Rector, and, as gunfire poured around them, he dragged him across the field, stopping occasionally to return fire. At the end of their move, Specialist Billings saw he had been dragging a dead man.

"Rector!" He snatched the medallion from his neck.

"S…Serge…!!!" Terrence beckoned desperately.

"Roger that Billings…Evans, I need you to get me all the air support you can get me on that mountain!" Sergeant Paniagua bellowed into Madison's ears.

"Yes, sir! Requesting close immediate air support! I need you to burn them out over on the hill top! ALPHA, BRAVO, coordinates 4-5-6-5!!!" Madison screamed into her radio, stopping to remind herself to breathe. With her eyes closed, she tried desperately to get her shaking hands under control. There was an explosion; it sent waves of terror piercing into her heart. She hid behind the large rock.

"O…O…Over on the hill top Bravo…4-5-7-2, I say again 4-5-7-2!!"

Soon air support poured in, setting fire to the mountain tops, blasting the enemies in an instant massacre. Sergeant Paniagua grabbed one side of the radio and Madison with the other.

"Top of the hill!!" he ordered.

"Move!! Move!!" Terrence bellowed.

Running. Shooting. Trying frantically to avoid the balls of fire that threatened to swallow them, and the stinging bullets from the barrels of the enemies' guns that threatened to pierce their hearts.

Explosions after explosions sent men flying like Frisbees. An object as heavy as a boulder hit Sergeant Paniagua straight in the back. It was the remains of a soldier with only his left leg and right arm attached to a torso. Madison dragged the corpse off of him and again the two were headed up the mountain, stopping occasionally to clear their way by killing one or two men who approached them.

At the top of the mountain, all seemed to be at peace, falling in surrender to their knees. Terrance and what was left of his team gazed down the side of the hill. Limbless, lifeless, maimed, mutilated corpses lie along the sides of the hill and at the base of the mountain. They looked around them desperately and saw they had made it. The gunfire ceased. The smoke and dirt that had been suspended in the air receded. Heart rates slowed in the realization.

There was a chuckle, then a laugh, then an uproar of cheers.

"We…we made it!" one screamed in a frenzied daze.

"I'm putting my gun into the ground!" another declared, removing his rifle from his body, while simultaneously dropping it and himself to his knees.

Terrence stood, dazed, lost, conflicted between a range of emotions, as he looked down on the number of comrades they had lost.

"She's been hit," he heard someone say....

"Madison," he called her name in a desperate whisper. "We made it! You hear me? No no...This is it! You can't do this! Not now!!"

Terrence clenched his teeth in a frustrated agonizing rage. His pulsating heartbeats tripped over each other, he couldn't contain himself. Hot, heavy, salty crystals fell in steady streams down his face, out of his reservoir as he could feel her life slipping away, out of his hands. He hugged her tighter, as if to try to prevent her soul from escaping from his grasp. His tears dropped to her face, washing away the blood that stained her cheeks.

He saw her gaze shift to him and, in one last attempt to speak, she murmured, "I love you."

Note from the Publisher

Are you a first time author?

Not sure how to proceed to get your book published?
Want to keep all your rights and all your royalties?
Want it to look as good as a Top 10 publisher?
Need help with editing, layout, cover design?
Want it out there selling in 90 days or less?

Visit our website for some exciting new options!

www.ingramcontent.com/pod-product-compliance
Lightning Source LLC
Chambersburg PA
CBHW051927220626
47052CB00003B/607